D1377920

PETAWAWA
PUBLIC LIBRARY

African Tales

Retold by Saviour Pirotta

Illustrated by Peter Kettle

WAYLAND

Traditional Stories

African Tales

Native American Tales

Editor: Cath Senker
Cover design: Dennis Day

First published in 1998 by Wayland Publishers Ltd,
61 Western Road, Hove, East Sussex, BN3 1JD, England

British Library Cataloguing in Publication Data
Pirotta, Saviour
African Tales. – Simplified ed. – (Traditional Stories)
I. Tales – Africa – Juvenile literature
I. Title II. Kettle, Peter, 1941– III. Hull, Robert.
African Stories
398.2'096

ISBN 0 7502 2272 7

Typeset by Cath Senker
Printed by...
Bound by...

This book is based on the original title *African Stories*, published in 1992 by Wayland Publishers Ltd.
Artwork by Peter Kettle.
Map artwork on page 47 by Peter Bull.

Contents

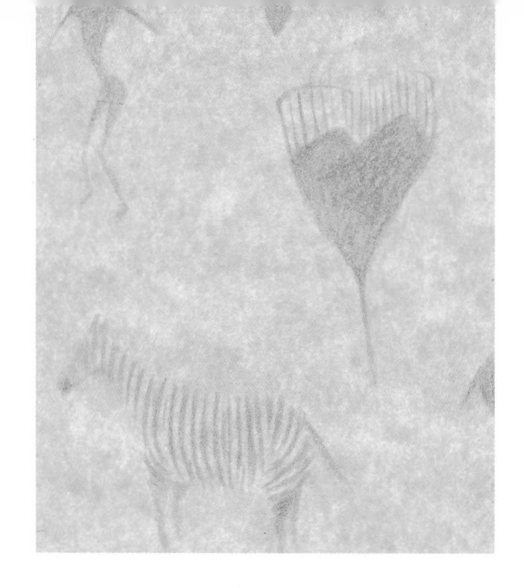

Introduction

Africa is the biggest continent in the world. It is made up of many different countries, all with their own cultures, languages and traditions.

Many Africans live in cities. Others inhabit the rain forest or farms and villages on the grasslands. In the north, there are Bedouin – people who spend their lives moving around the desert regions.

There are different religions in Africa too. The people of North Africa are mostly Muslims. Many people in Central Africa and the South believe in either Christianity or Animism, an ancient African faith.

It all makes for a rich variety of life that is reflected in the thousands of stories that are told on this vast continent. The Africans have many creation stories that explain the beginning of the world and the arrival of human beings on Earth.

They also have short folk tales that are meant to teach children important things about life and society. Some stories are told to make people laugh, others to make the listeners cry. There are trickster tales, animal tales, legends, fairy tales and ghost stories guaranteed to keep you awake at night.

In the evening, after the animals have been locked in their pens and supper has been eaten, many village people gather round the fire to listen to stories. In North Africa, women and children sit around the storyteller while the men are out at the coffee house. They ply the storyteller with sweets and tea to make her tell more and more stories.

Many of these tales have never been written down. Most of them are passed on from father to son, from mother to daughter. But many others have found their way into books, and into the hearts and minds of children around the world.

These are only a handful of them.

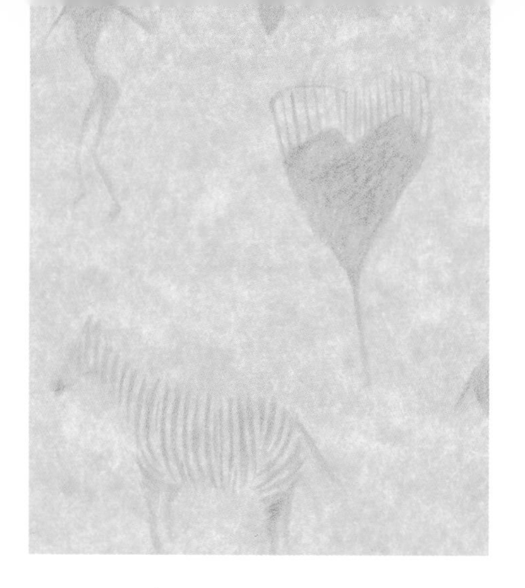

A holy cat

Animals appear in hundreds of stories. Sometimes, as in this story from North Africa, they act like people.

The cat who went to Mecca

Once there was a nasty cat who liked eating mice. One day he said to his friends, 'I am going on the pilgrimage to Mecca.'

His friends were astonished.

'But you're bad,' they said. 'Only holy people go to Mecca.'

'I'm going to turn over a new leaf,' said the horrible cat. And he put on his sandals and marched down the road.

Three months later he came back.

'We should pay him a visit,' said the chief mouse to his fellow mice. 'One should always congratulate pilgrims returning from Mecca.'

'Be careful,' said the mice. 'He'll gobble you up.'

'Perhaps he's changed,' said the old mouse. 'You can't possibly go on the pilgrimage and come back the same as you were before.'

He crept out of his mousehole and went to see the cat.

The cat was reading the Qu'ran. He was wearing a white cap, to show that he had been to Mecca.

'Welcome back home,' said the old mouse.

'Thank you,' said the cat, offering the mouse some dates. 'Please, do not be afraid of me. I do not eat mice any more.'

'Praise be to Allah,' cried the mouse. 'You really have changed.'

A few days later, the cat went for a walk. When he reached the pond he saw some young mice.

'Hello,' squeaked two of the mice, 'we heard you don't eat our kind any more.'

The cat nodded, trying hard to smile. But then he couldn't help himself. His eyes started to water and he drooled. With a loud snarl he pounced on the two mice and gobbled them up.

The rest of the mice fled. 'We'll never trust a cat again,' they said, 'for even a cat who's been to Mecca is still a cat.'

Two sisters

In Somalia, children are allowed to stay up after dark to listen to stories around the fire. This is one of their favourites.

A question of marriage

Once there were two sisters. One was beautiful and stupid. The other was plain but clever. One day a young man came to their village looking for a wife. At first he couldn't take his eyes off the beautiful sister. Then he talked to the plain one. She didn't dazzle him like her sibling but she talked a lot of sense.

The man was confused. 'What should I go for,' he wondered, 'beauty or intelligence?' He decided to go and see Kabacalaf, the wise man of the village. Kabacalaf said, 'Ask both sisters three questions. The one who gives you the right answers shall be your bride.'

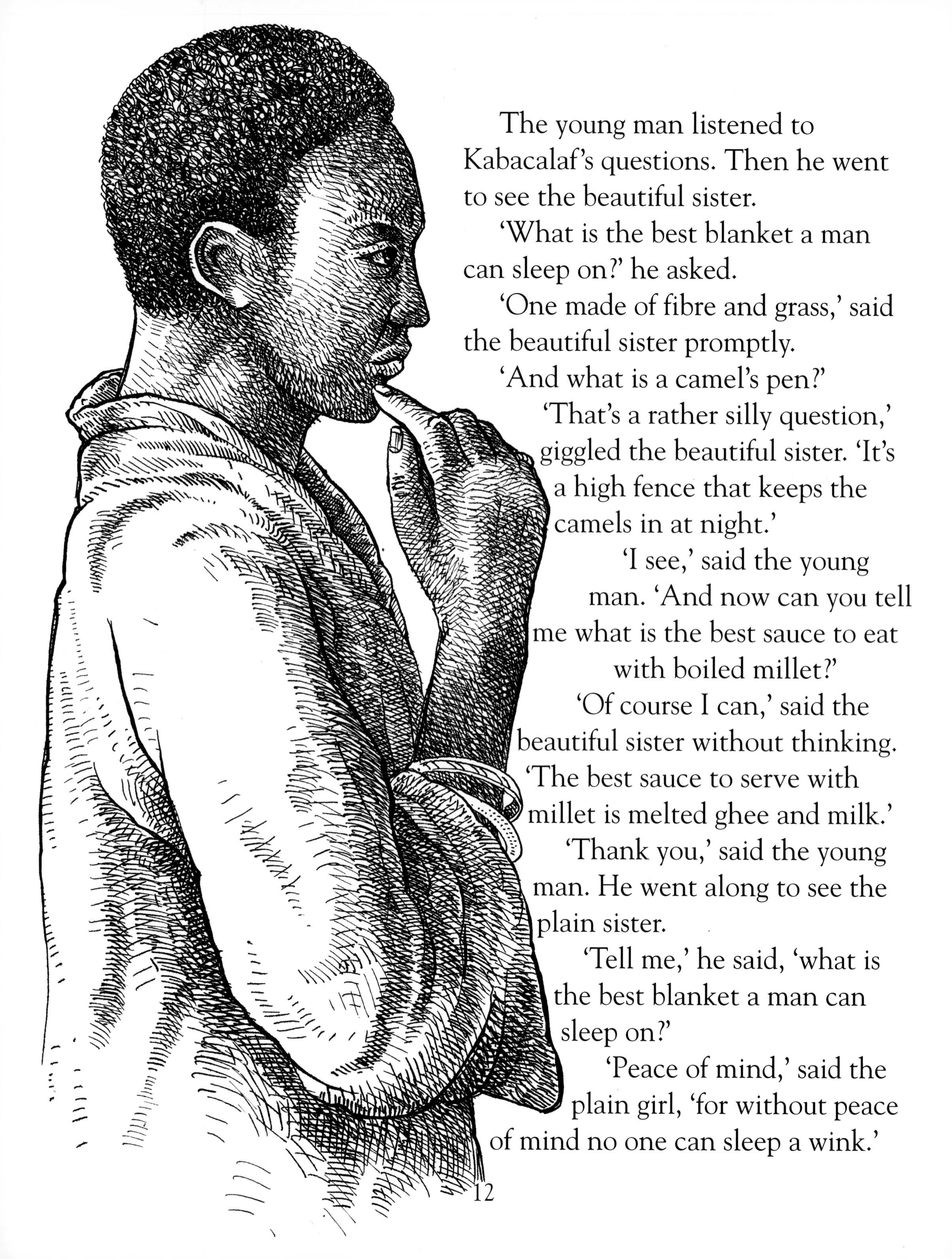

The young man listened to Kabacalaf's questions. Then he went to see the beautiful sister.

'What is the best blanket a man can sleep on?' he asked.

'One made of fibre and grass,' said the beautiful sister promptly.

'And what is a camel's pen?'

'That's a rather silly question,' giggled the beautiful sister. 'It's a high fence that keeps the camels in at night.'

'I see,' said the young man. 'And now can you tell me what is the best sauce to eat with boiled millet?'

'Of course I can,' said the beautiful sister without thinking. 'The best sauce to serve with millet is melted ghee and milk.'

'Thank you,' said the young man. He went along to see the plain sister.

'Tell me,' he said, 'what is the best blanket a man can sleep on?'

'Peace of mind,' said the plain girl, 'for without peace of mind no one can sleep a wink.'

'What is a camel's pen?' asked the young man.

'A camel's pen is man himself, for it is man who herds the camels together for safety at night.'

'And what is the best sauce to serve with boiled millet?' came the last question.

The plain sister thought for a while. Then she said, 'The best sauce to serve with millet is hunger because when you are hungry everything tastes delicious.'

The young man was most impressed with her answers. She had spoken most wisely.

Now he knew what his decision would be. He realized that the plain sister would make a caring, wonderful companion who would share his problems and give him advice. So he asked her to marry him – and she agreed.

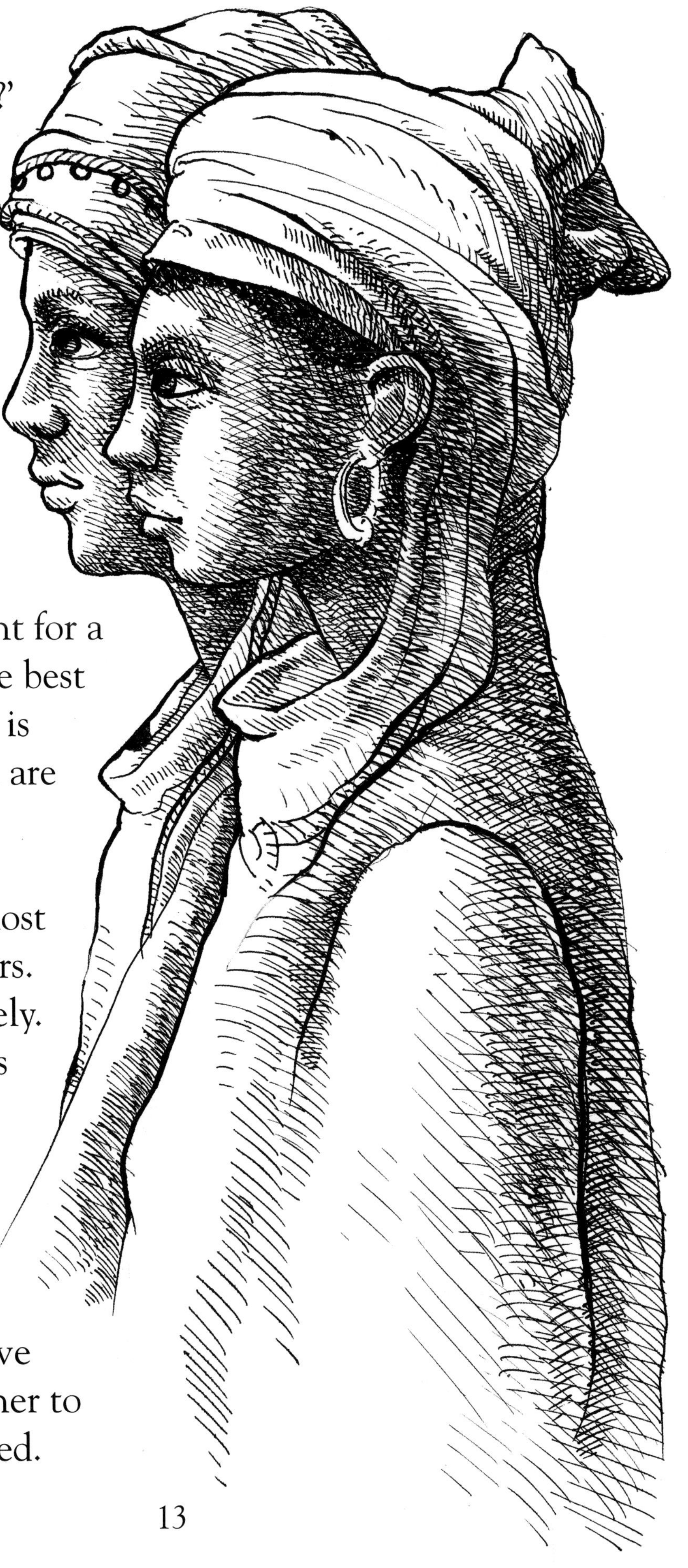

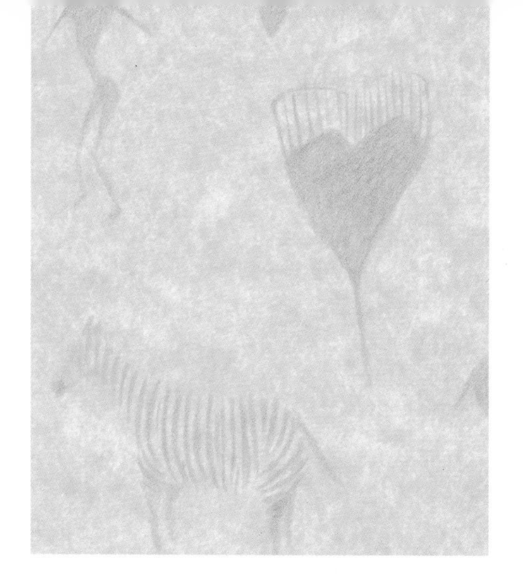

Chameleon and hare

This story is from southern Africa.

Why people die

Shortly after God had made the first people, he called for Chameleon.

'Go tell the people,' said God, 'that they will never die. When their time on Earth is over, they shall go away and then return frequently, like the moon.'

Chameleon was the wisest of the world's creatures. He knew that God's message was of the utmost importance, so he memorized it carefully. Only then did he set off to find the first people.

It was a slow journey. Chameleon stopped often, to eat and rest. He was careful which paths he took. To protect himself from wild animals, he kept changing his colour to match his surroundings. That made it difficult for anyone to see him.

God started to worry. When was Chameleon going to deliver his message? Perhaps the poor animal had died in the woods?

God decided to send a second messenger. He called Hare, who was fast on his legs and could outrun the wind.

'Go tell the people,' said God, 'that when their time on Earth is over they shall not die. Instead, they shall return to Earth frequently, like the moon.'

Hare listened to God's message. Then he tore off in search of the first people. He bounded across deserts, shot across plains and swam across oceans. On the way he passed Chameleon but he did not notice him. He was in far too much of a hurry.

Hare reached the first people, who had set up camp on the edge of a forest.

'I have a message from God,' he said.

'What is it?' cried the people. 'Tell us please, quickly!'

Hare cleared his throat. He'd been in such a hurry to leave God that he hadn't listened to the message properly. He'd forgotten most of it. But he couldn't tell that to the people. They might be angry with him.

'It's something about death,' he said.

'Now let me see . . . Yes, when you die, you shall not return to Earth. You shall be gone for ever.'

The people screamed. Some beat their chests and wailed. Hare realized he'd got the message all wrong. But there was nothing he could do now. Once the words of God were spoken, they could not be altered. So he sniffed and bounded off into the forest.

Some time later Chameleon reached the first people. He was shocked when he heard what Hare had said. But he could not alter the message now. It was cast in stone.

Chameleon was kind. He decided to stay with the people and comfort them. He would teach them how to be wise like him. He would show them how to tread carefully, how to think before taking important decisions. That way they would live as long as possible.

KETTLE

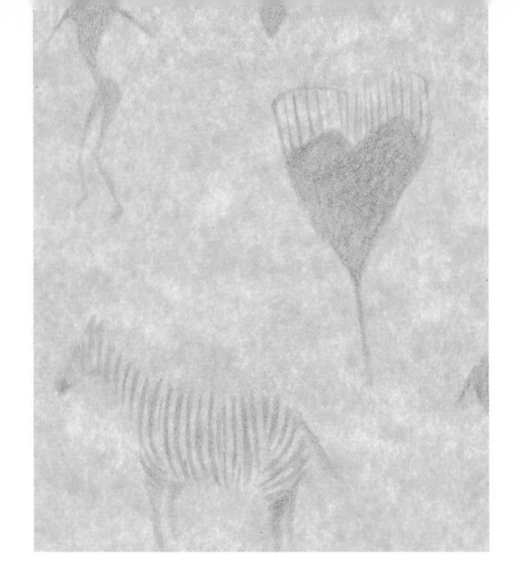

Ata-okolo-inona

Madagascar is an enormous island off the east coast of Africa. This story is told in the south-western part of the island, where there is very little rain.

Creation of death and rain

Soon after Ndrian-ana-hary, the Great Spirit, had finished making the Earth, he called for Ata-okolo-inona, his son.

'Go down to Earth,' he ordered, 'and tell me what you see there. If the planet is good enough, I shall fill it with living creatures.'

Ata-okolo-inona travelled down from the skies. He arrived just before dawn, when the air was nice and cool.

Ata-okolo-inona liked Earth very much. It was a bit dry. There was sand everywhere. Bare rocks jutted out of a small lake. But the air was clear. That was a good thing.

Soon the sun came up. Ata-okolo-inona started to sweat. He had never felt such fierce heat before. The blazing sun burnt his skin. His mind reeled. He looked for shelter but there were no trees yet, no shrubs.

'What shall I do?' thought Ata-okolo-inona. He wandered around the dry land, thinking. At last he noticed that the ground under his feet was soft. So he started digging – a nice, dark tunnel would shield him from the fierce sun.

It took Ata-okolo-inona a long time to finish the tunnel. But, at last, he had a cool place to rest in. He shut his eyes. Soon he had drifted into a long, deep sleep . . .

Years passed. Ata-okolo-inona slept on, sheltered in his cool hiding place. Up in the heavens, the Great Spirit started to worry. 'Where is my son?' he wondered. 'Is he lost? Has he met some misfortune?'

He wanted to go down to Earth and look for him but he couldn't leave his place in the heavens. Someone had to make sure that the stars twinkled and the moon shone at the right time.

So the Great Spirit sent his servants to look for Ata-okolo-inona.

'Do not come back,' he said, 'until you have found my son.'

The Great Spirit's servants came to Earth. They wandered around, blinded by the fierce sun. Some looked for Ata-okolo-inona in the desert and some searched the hills, but they could not find him.

At last they decided to send a man to see Ndrian-ana-hary. 'Tell the Great Spirit that we cannot find his son,' they said. 'What shall we do next?'

The man hurried up into the sky. But he never came back. The servants sent more and more people to see the Great Spirit but none of them returned either.

The servants were confused. What should they do? Where could they search? Up in the sky, Ndrian-ana-hary wanted the servants to keep on looking until they found his son. To help them, he decided to make Earth a better place to live. So he sent the rains. Soon the sea was bigger. Rivers appeared, and fish and birds and animals came to the forests. The Earth was greener.

The servants were happier now. They had become the first people. The Earth was their new home.

To this very day, the people keep sending messengers to ask the Great Spirit where to look for Ata-okolo-inona. The messengers never return. They are the dead.

KETTLE

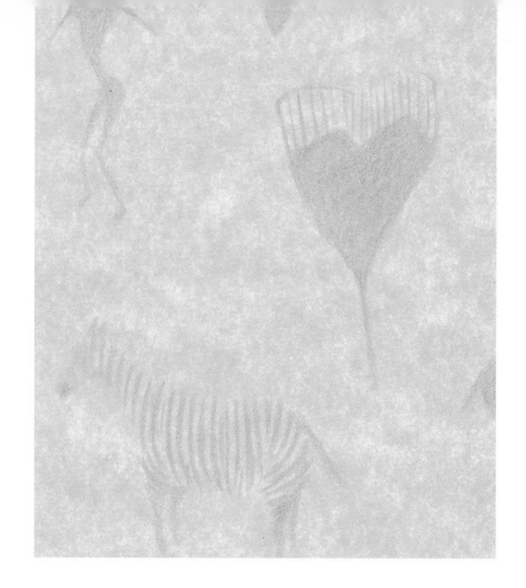

The kid goat

This story comes from Ethiopia.

The young girl was supposed to be looking after her father's goats. But she fell asleep. When she woke up, she counted the flock. All the adults were there. But three of the kids were missing.

The girl panicked. She knew her father would be very angry if she went home without the kids. So, calling the rest of the flock to her, she set out to find them.

'Have you seen my kids?' she asked everyone she met. No one had seen them. The girl hurried on, tears welling in her eyes.

'Have you seen three lost kids?' she asked a young man sitting near a fig tree. The young man was deaf. He thought the girl was asking him the way to the water-hole.

'Over there,' he said, pointing past the tree. 'Behind the prickly pears.'

KETTLE

The girl hurried to the water-hole and there, frightened and bleating, were the missing kids. One of them had hurt its foot.

'There you are!' said the girl. She picked up the injured kid and called the others to her.

On the way back she met the man again.

'Thank you very much,' she said.

'That's all right,' said the man, thinking the girl was grateful to him for pointing out the water-hole.

'Would you like this injured kid?' she asked. 'Perhaps you can look after it better than I can.'

The man thought the girl was accusing him of injuring the kid.

'No, no,' he said, backing away from her, 'it wasn't me.'

'Of course it was you,' said the girl, puzzled. 'Here, take the kid.'

'But it wasn't me,' said the man. 'I never went anywhere near the water-hole.'

'Still, you knew the kids were there,' insisted the girl.

The man's face turned a bright red. 'Leave me alone,' he shouted.

A crowd gathered round the man and the girl. 'What's going on here?' asked an old farmer.

'I want to give this man a present,' said the girl, 'but he won't take it.'

'This girl's hassling me,' complained the man. 'She won't leave me alone.' He was so upset that he started waving his walking stick around.

'Watch out,' said the farmer. 'You're going to hit someone with that stick.' But it was too late. The deaf man accidentally hit the girl on the arms. The kid fell to the ground.

'I'm going to report you to the judge,' cried the girl. 'You hit me and made me drop an injured kid.'

'I only hit her by mistake,' said the man to the crowd.

The girl marched straight to the local judge's house, followed by the crowd and her goats. The deaf man went along too, ready to defend himself.

'What do you want?' called the judge from the bedroom window. He had just woken up from his afternoon nap and he couldn't find his glasses.

'That brute hit me,' said the girl, pointing to the deaf man. 'I only hit her by accident,' the deaf man defended himself. 'She accused me of injuring her kid.'

The judge couldn't make head nor tail of the situation. He had a terrible headache

and the goats were bleating loud enough to wake the dead. But he knew what to do. Most of the people who came to see him were husbands and wives who'd just had a row. These two seemed to be no different. If he talked to them gravely enough, they'd think he knew what was going on.

'Silence!' he roared. Everyone stopped talking right away.

'All this quarrelling between couples in the village is a disgrace,' proclaimed the judge. He turned to the deaf man.

'As for you,' he said, 'you must stop mistreating your wife at once.'

'But . . .' said the deaf man.

'No buts,' growled the judge, turning to the girl. 'While you, make sure you take your husband his lunch in time.' He blinked at the kid in her arms which he thought was a baby. 'As for this young child, may it teach us all to live in peace and harmony.'

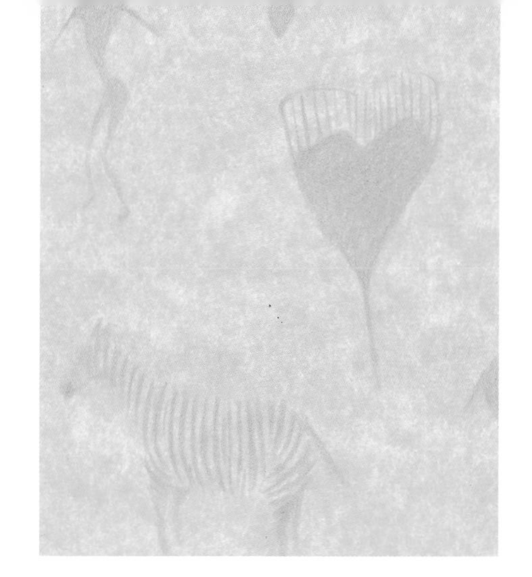

The severed head

This story comes from West Africa, though other versions are told around the African continent.

The merchant and the head

The merchant was walking along the forest path. Suddenly he saw something that made his blood run cold. It was a man's head, sitting on top of a tree-stump.

The merchant stopped to look at it. The head had been chopped off at the neck. It was bleeding.

Suddenly the swollen lips moved. 'Don't say anything,' hissed the head.

The poor merchant bolted for his life. He didn't stop running till he came to a town. 'Perhaps I should tell the king what I have seen,' he thought. 'He might give me a reward.'

P KETTLE

So he went to the king's palace.

'What do you want?' asked one of the guards outside the front gate.

'I have an important message for His Majesty,' said the merchant.

'Follow me,' said the guard. He led the merchant into a chamber where the king was discussing affairs of state with his chiefs.

'What is it?' asked the king.

'This man says he has an urgent message for you,' replied the guard. The king looked at the merchant. 'This had better be important,' he said. 'You've interrupted an urgent meeting.'

'I'm sorry,' mumbled the merchant. 'But I saw a severed head on the outskirts of your town. I thought you might like to know about it.'

The king glared. 'Is that all?'

'No,' said the merchant. 'The head talked to me. It spoke.'

'Did it now?' sneered the king.

'It did, honestly,' said the merchant.

'In that case,' said the king, 'I'll send some guards to fetch it to the palace.'

He turned to the guards. 'Go with him,' he ordered. 'If the head speaks, bring it back to me and I'll give this man a big reward. If it doesn't, chop off his head and leave it there.'

The merchant was not at all scared about having his head chopped off. He was sure the severed head had spoken to him. It would speak again, in front of the guards. He would get his just reward.

The guards went with him to the forest. They inspected the head. 'Hurry up,' they said, 'make it talk.'

'Speak to me, head,' said the merchant.

The severed head remained silent.

'Say something to the king's guards,' begged the merchant.

The head looked like it had an evil smile on its lips. But it refused to speak.

'You were lying,' said the chief guard. He lifted his axe and chopped off the merchant's head. It rolled on to the grass.

'Poor man,' said the guards.

Behind them there was a snigger.

'I told him not to say anything,' whispered the head on the tree-stump.

For a moment, the guards froze. Then they ran for their lives.

Nogwaja

Hare features in many African stories. He has different names in different countries. In Zulu tales, he is called Nogwaja, the Mischief Maker. Here is a story that shows how he became the cleverest trickster in the world.

How Nogwaja gained his cunning

Once there was a drought. Only Elephant had some water left in her water-hole and she wouldn't share it with anyone. It was strictly for her family only.

'I'm going to trick Elephant out of her water,' boasted Nogwaja to the other animals.

'You're not clever enough to do that,' they said.

'Oh yeah?' Nogwaja replied. 'You'll see.'

Nogwaja went to see Honeyguide, a little bird that was very good at getting honey from bees' nests. 'Give me some of your honey,' he said, 'and I'll get you some of Elephant's water.'

Honeyguide gave Nogwaja a calabash full of fresh honey. Nogwaja took it to Elephant. 'Hello, Elephant,' he said, 'would you like some sweet, yellow water?'

Elephant had some of the honey. 'It tastes much better than my water,' she cried, smacking her lips. 'Where did you get it?'

'From a secret water-hole,' lied Nogwaja, 'but I'm afraid it's too far away from here for an elephant to reach.'

Elephant was rather offended by Nogwaja's remark. 'Tell me where it is,' she said, 'and I'll show you if I can get there or not.'

Nogwaja pointed to a mountain. 'It's right at the foot of that mountain,' he whispered, 'in a deep, dark water-hole. But don't tell anyone else about it. The others might want some sweet water too.'

'Don't worry,' chuckled Elephant, 'your secret is safe with me.' She gathered her family around her and set out to find the yellow water-hole at once. Nogwaja waited till they had walked away. Then he started drinking from Elephant's water-hole.

'Hey, leave some for me!' said Honeyguide. Nogwaja shook his head. 'Go away, stupid bird,' he said. 'This water's all mine.'

Honeyguide was furious. 'We'll see about that,' she said. She flew towards the mountain and caught up with Elephant.

'Nogwaja has tricked you,' she said. 'There is no secret water-hole. That liquid you drank was my honey.'

Elephant was livid. She charged back to the water-hole, caught Nogwaja in her trunk and hurled him into a thorny bush.

'You're not so clever really, are you?' said the animals to Nogwaja.

Nogwaja was most embarrassed. He went away and hid in the woods. All day long, he wondered how he could become more cunning. In the end he decided to ask the Spirits. They were powerful, and they could help him to become the cleverest animal in the world.

First Nogwaja went to see Wind. 'Can you help me become clever?' he asked. Wind blew gently around him and ruffled his fur, but he did not reply.

Next Nogwaja paid a visit to River. 'Will you teach me how to be cunning?' he asked the rippling water. River refused to speak. She went on bubbling and gurgling, stepping gingerly over the stones in her path.

Then Nogwaja approached Sun. 'Will you help me to become cunning?' he begged. Sun ignored him too. She was far too busy showing off her radiance.

Nogwaja felt like giving up. He was so miserable he could not sleep at night. He lay by his burrow, weeping. That's when he saw Moon. 'Moon,' he cried, 'will you make me cleverer than all the creatures in the world?'

Moon was hanging above a mountain, too far away to hear Nogwaja's request.

'I must get closer to her,' said Nogwaja. 'I must learn to jump straight into the sky.'

He started practising right away. He jumped over stones, he jumped over boulders. In no time at all, he could jump right over a tree.

The next time Moon hung low in the sky, Hare jumped towards her. The animals could see his shadow right across her face. They could see him talking and nodding, drinking in her every word.

What did Moon tell Nogwaja? No one knows, but when he came back, he still had a glint of moonlight in his eyes. He kept away from the other animals, only coming out of his burrow to play mischief on other creatures. Now he was really clever; no one could match his cunning.

To this very day, Nogwaja still visits Moon for her advice. If you look up to the sky at night, you can see his dark shape set against her silver face.

Ghosts

In the Congo ghosts are living skeletons. They live in caves or abandoned houses. Most grow the thumbnail on their right hand into a long, sharp knife. It comes in handy when they want to carve up human flesh.

The hunter and the ghost

The hunter was tired. He'd been hunting for days and he was dying to get back home. But it was getting dark. And the antelope slung over his shoulder was getting very heavy.

'Shall we stop for the night?' the hunter asked his two dogs.

The dogs barked. They'd already spotted a small house by the road. It was surrounded by tall weeds. 'Looks like no one's home,' joked the hunter. He pushed the door open. Just as he had thought, the place was deserted. The hunter tied the dead antelope to a beam in

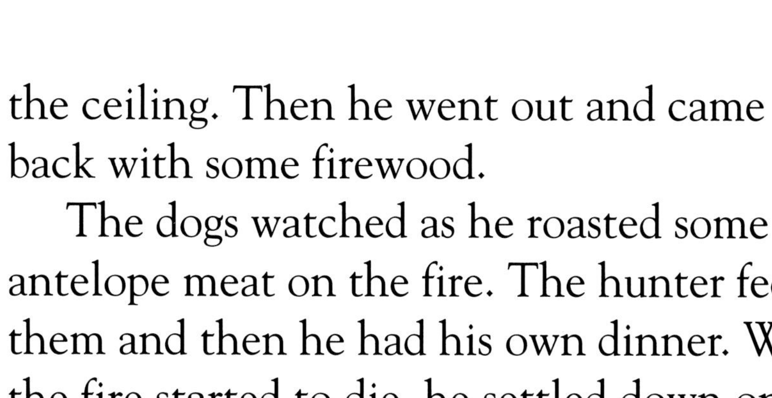

the ceiling. Then he went out and came back with some firewood.

The dogs watched as he roasted some antelope meat on the fire. The hunter fed them and then he had his own dinner. When the fire started to die, he settled down on the floor. The dogs snuggled up to him. Soon the three of them were lost to the world.

An hour or so later the door to the hut creaked open. A ghost stood in the doorway, his bones glowing white in the moonlight.

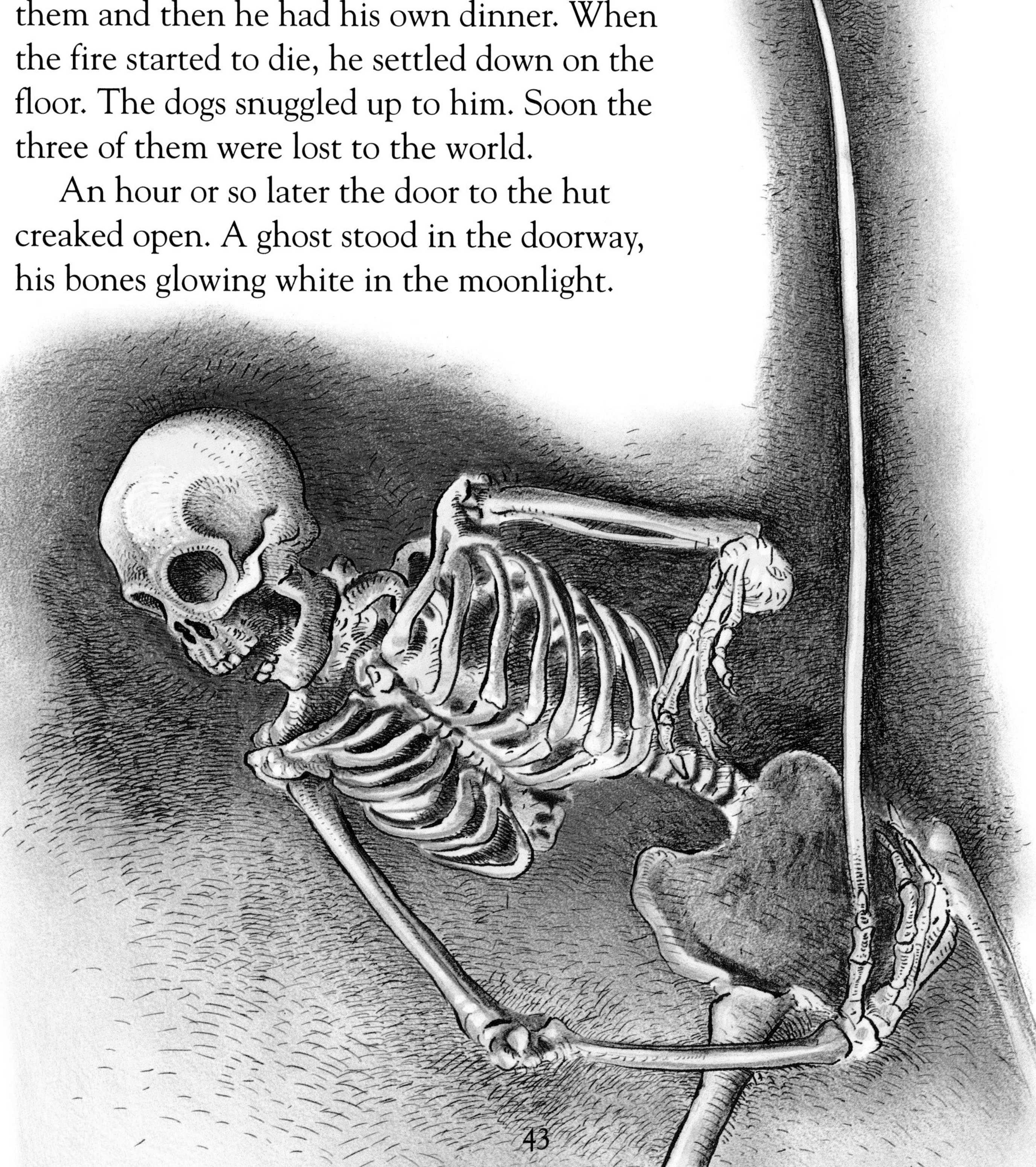

The ghost saw the man and the dogs. He frowned. 'How dare they invade my home?' he muttered darkly. 'This hut is mine. I've been living here since the people who built it moved away.'

He thought about giving the three a horrible scare. Then he had a better idea. He would have them for dinner. His walk in the forest had made him hungry, ravenous even. Some people think ghosts do not eat. But that's not true. African ghosts have a healthy appetite. They eat anything they can sink their rotting teeth in, especially human flesh.

The ghost grinned. He would eat the man first. Human flesh was tasty, better than dog meat. He moved to the dying fire and held his sharpened thumbnail in the embers. It hurt a bit but he didn't mind. You needed to heat up your nail if you wanted to cut raw flesh. You wanted your nail to be sharp, like a real knife.

The ghost gazed at the sleeping hunter. 'Which part of him should I have first?' he wondered. 'Should I start with a plump arm, a leg, or the juicy belly?'

The dogs squirmed in their sleep. One of them yelped faintly, as if she was chasing a rabbit in her dreams.

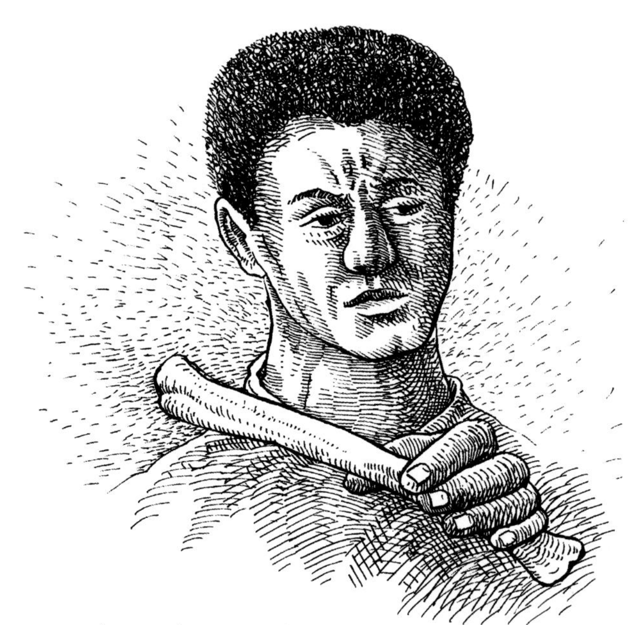

The ghost drooled. When he'd finished with the hunter, he'd eat the dogs . . .

The ghost gasped. He'd left his thumbnail in the fire too long. It was burning. He backed away from the fire, shaking his nail in the air. Like other ghosts, he couldn't smell a thing but he knew the hut must be filled with the stink of burning bone. He had to get out before he was discovered.

Just then the dogs woke up. They glared at the ghost, their fur standing on end. The ghost lunged at the door but it was too late. With a fierce growl, the dogs were on him. Bleached bones went flying everywhere. The ghost's skull clattered to the floor.

The din woke up the hunter. 'What's the matter, dogs?' he asked, rubbing the sleep out of his eyes. The dogs did not reply. They were far too busy licking the ghost's nice, juicy bones.

Notes

Ata-okolo-inona (pp20–24)
The son of Ndrian-ana-hary, the Great Spirit, in a Madagascan story of the creation of the world.

Calabash (p37)
The shell of a gourd or pumpkin. It is used as a food bowl.

Chameleon (pp14–18)
A kind of lizard that lives in most African countries. It can change colour to match its surroundings.

Elephant (pp36–41)
In African stories the elephant is the wise chief who settles arguments among the animals.

Honeyguide (pp37–8)
A small bird that leads other animals to bees' nests. After the animals have taken the honey the honeyguide eats beeswax, bees, larvae and any remaining honey.

Kabacalaf (pp11–13)
A wise man who appears in many Somali stories.

Mecca (p6)
The most important place for Muslims to visit on a pilgrimage. It is in Saudi Arabia.

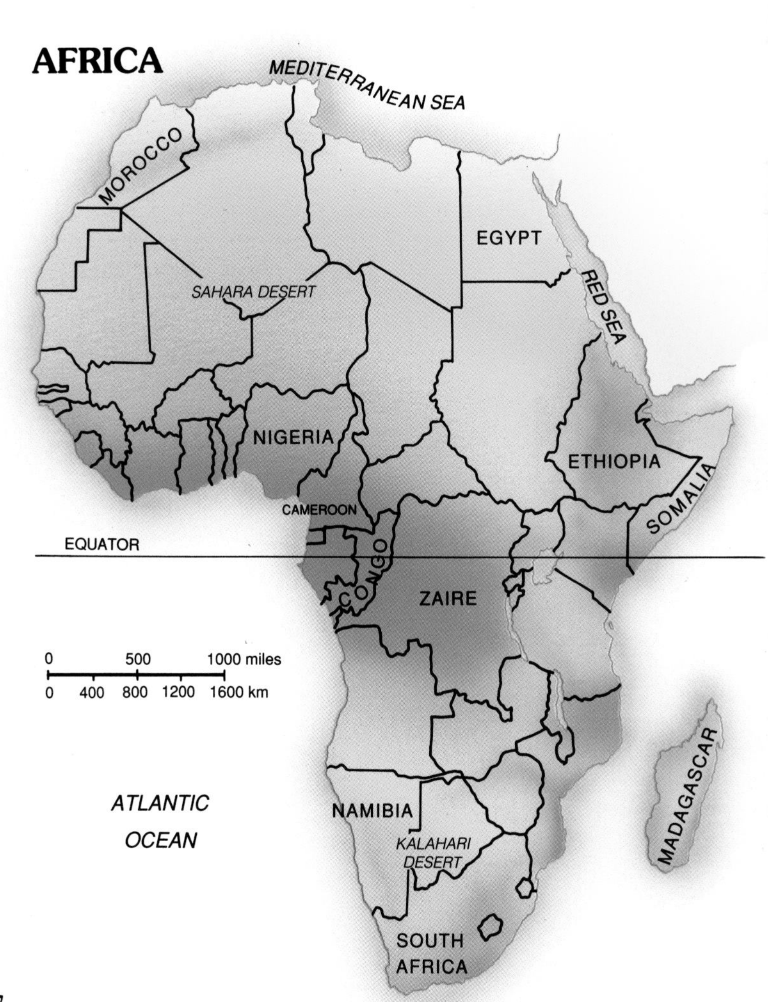

Moon (pp40–41)
The moon is important in stories and in some African religions too. In Namibia hunters blow an antelope horn to greet the moon.

Qu'ran (p10)
The sacred book of Muslims, believed to be the word of God.

Somalia (p11)
The Somali people live not only in Somalia itself but are also scattered throughout neighbouring African countries. They are well known for their poetry as well as for their stories.

Sun (p40)
The sun is sometimes a god in African stories, whom people may visit.

Zulu (p36)
The Zulu live in the south-east of South Africa. Like the Somali people, they are known for their poetry as well as for their stories.

Further reading

Classic African Children's Stories: A Collection of Ancient Tales by Phyllis Savory (Citadel, 1996)
Oxford Myths and Legends: West African Trickster Tales by Martin Bennett (Oxford University Press, 1994)
River that Went to the Sky: Tales by African Storytellers by Mary Medlicott (Kingfisher, 1995)
Tortoise and Other Animals: A Collection of Retold African Tales by J. Gbenga Fagborun (Virgocap, 1995)